HARVEST

GEORGE ANCONA

MARSHALL CAVENDISH · NEW YORK

Marshall Cavendish
99 White Plains Road
Tarrytown, New York 10951

Library of Congress Cataloging-in-Publication Data
Ancona, George.
Harvest / George Ancona.
   p. cm.
ISBN 0-7614-5086-6
1. Migrant agricultural laborers—United States—Juvenile
literature. [1. Migrant labor. 2. Alien labor.] I. Title.
HD1525.A63 2001
331.5'44'0973—dc21
2001017497

The text of this book is set in 12 point Bookman
Printed in Hong Kong
First Edition

6 5 4 3 2

To Michael Stearns

At 4:30 in the morning a man waits under a lamppost in the darkness of a deserted supermarket parking lot in Salinas, California. The shadowy figures of other men and women arrive from the dark and empty streets to gather in the shelter of the closed market. It is mid-August, yet the people are bundled against the cold that comes in from the Pacific Ocean. These are the farm workers, called *campesinos* in Spanish, who have come to *harvest* the crops that grow in the rich earth of the Salinas Valley.

Each worker carries a lunch in a shopping bag or backpack. The women's heads are wrapped with bandannas and a cap that leave only their eyes showing. Hairpins keep the scarves from blocking their vision. The bandannas protect them from the sun, dust, and *pesticides* in the fields.

Soon headlights sweep across the waiting farm workers and a bus comes to a stop. On a trailer behind it are two portable toilets and jugs of drinking water. The *campesinos* crowd around the labor contractor who has come to pick a crew. In Spanish he says, "I've got peppers to pick and need twenty pickers today. Who wants to work?" Then he tells them what he will pay—either by the hour or by the box, called piecework. Those who accept the terms board the bus.

More buses arrive. The remaining *campesinos* greet each bus in the hope of being chosen. Today is a good day. Everybody gets a job.

Most farm workers are *migrant* workers. They travel north from farm to farm to farm harvesting the crops as they ripen. On the East Coast workers flow from Florida north to Maine. A central stream starts in Texas and moves up through the Mid-Western states. In the West the migration begins in southern California and goes north to the state of Washington.

Mexican workers need permits to enter the United States. Those without papers have to sneak across. The people who guide them for a fee are called *coyotes*. Many *campesinos* get lost and die trying to cross the deserts. The workers come here because they earn in one day what they would earn in one week back home—if they could find a job.

Some workers find places to live in neighborhoods where people will rent them space in their home, their garage, or a trailer parked in the driveway. Farmers rent bunks in barracks near the fields. Workers without money sleep in shanties, in caves, or under bridges.

Raul and Teresa Ayala come every year to pick strawberries. They fly in from Mexico with their two children and live in a state-run migrant worker camp. The family arrives in May and returns in November.

At 5:30 in the morning Raul and Teresa prepare their lunch. Teresa is proud of the fresh *tortillas* she makes each morning. As Teresa cooks tortillas on the *comal*, Raul fills them with meat and sauce and rolls them into *burritos*. Then he wraps them in tinfoil and puts them into a wide-mouthed thermos to keep warm.

The family leaves by six and drops off the children at school. Raul and Teresa begin work at seven. They usually work ten hours a day, six days a week, but sometimes go on as long as fourteen hours. Raul has been picking strawberries for nineteen years.

7

Strawberry picking is stoop labor. A picker must work bent over all day. The best time to pick is early in the season when the plants have few leaves and you can see the berries. Later in the season the plants fill out with leaves and the picker has to search for the hidden berries. A picker picks only the ripe strawberries, and leaves the others to ripen.

He puts the strawberries into plastic containers in a flat box. The box lies on a low wheelbarrow that the picker pushes along. Before each container is closed the best berries are arranged on top to look pretty. Every picker has a card tucked into his or her cap. When the flat is filled, the worker takes it to a *checker* who punches the card. The workers are paid by how many flats they fill.

At one end of a strawberry field a sign warns of *pesticides*. Strawberries are heavily sprayed and workers often get sick. Women wear masks and gloves to protect themselves, but men don't. As they work the pickers joke with each other to make the work easier to bear. The only way to know when a woman picker is smiling is to look for the crinkles around her eyes.

When Teresa and Raul return from the fields they remove their outer clothes to avoid bringing pesticides into the house.

During the morning, a mist wets the workers' clothes. When the mists clear, the sun dries them off. The cold, the dampness, and the heat get into their bones and their muscles and joints begin to ache. Teresa's back hurts and she does not think she can continue to work in the fields much longer.

Because he has worked for one grower for many years Raul and his family have medical insurance. Most field workers don't. And many do not try to get medical help when they get sick, because they can't afford it or because they don't have the proper papers and might get deported.

11

In a lettuce field a gigantic packing machine with tow arms slowly moves along the rows of lettuce. Far ahead of the machine men pick the rows that will be crushed by the machine's wheels. The picker cuts the lettuce from the root, trims it and puts each head into a plastic bag. After a carton is filled, another man comes along and staples it closed.

Another crew works close to the machine. Men and women pick lettuce and pass it to a packer at the conveyor belt. When a box is full it moves along the belt, where it is closed and loaded onto a waiting truck. Over the heads of the packers are the men who unfold and open the boxes for the packers.

Every crew is supervised by a foreman called *el mayordomo*. He hires the crew and tells them when to start and stop working. He also makes sure that the crew picks the right quality of produce. The crew is paid by contract, which means that the field is picked for a set price that the crew shares equally. The pickers work very quickly to finish the job fast. This is how they can make more money by the hour.

Fashion is very important to the women field workers. The kerchiefs they wear over their faces and hair are pretty. Each tries to embroider her own design on the kerchief that hangs down her back. Shirts tied around their waists create a half-skirt behind them.

Un Domingo en San Felipe, Baja California fue la última vez que estuve con mis padres. Fue el día más triste para mí, porque después de 20 años de convivir día y noche con ellos, tuvé que separarme para venir a Salinas para estar con mi esposo.

14

A migrant program in Salinas, California provides children with a place to stay while their parents work. In the evening parents also attend school to study English. With their children they take part in projects that preserve Mexican traditions such a making *piñatas*. They can also join a choral group or take computer courses. Members of a writing group create books that tell their stories. Bernice Gomez made a book that reveals her feelings in her new country.

O*ne Sunday in San Felipe in Lower California was the last time I was with my parents. It was the saddest day for me, because I had to leave them to come to Salinas to be with my husband. My husband came here first and was alone for one and a half years. He would return to San Felipe to*

visit. My mother insisted that I follow him since we were recently married and now had a daughter.

At first I worked in the field harvesting lettuce. I got the job because my father-in-law was the mayordomo *of the crew. On the first days I worked for fourteen and sixteen hours. I learned fast but it was hard. I lasted only two months and then I got a fever. Now since I have the two children I don't work in the fields any more. My husband drives a tractor.*

My hopes for my children are that they work and study hard to become someone important, that they have self-esteem, that they have principles, and that they be useful to society. My husband is becoming a citizen and my papers are being prepared. We are alone here and struggling but thanks to God we are doing well.

Green peppers are another crop that people have to stoop down to pick. At one end of the field a machine with a conveyor belt drops the peppers into a large crate. When the crate is full a tractor takes the peppers to a packing plant.

Each picker moves along a row of plants searching for ripe peppers. When a five gallon bucket is filled the picker takes it and

spills the peppers onto the conveyor belt. Women sort the peppers for size and quality.

The Salinas Valley is an ancient riverbed. That's why the soil is so rich. The river brings nutrients from the mountains. The valley has a good climate for growing cool-weather crops such as lettuce, broccoli, peppers, and artichokes.

17

Broccoli is picked by a crew from Mexico who travel and work together every season. As the machine inches its way down the field, the crew follows, cutting ripe heads of broccoli off the plants and tossing them onto trays on the packing machine. The men above pack the broccoli into cartons. With these machines the produce can be picked and packed right on the field and then trucked directly to customers. Hanging on the machine among the lunch bags is a portable radio that plays Latin music to accompany the gossip, jokes, and comments of the pickers.

Harvesting celery is the toughest job in the fields. As the giant packing machine creeps down the field, men in front of it work swiftly with sharp square-end knives. First the *campesino* stabs the base of the celery plant to cut it from the root. With the stalk in his left hand he squares off the base, then flips it to lop off the top of the celery. Then he drops the trimmed stalk to the ground and reaches for the next plant.

Between the cutter and the machine is another man who drops the celery into a plastic bag and packs it into a carton. Above the conveyor belt another crew staples the boxes shut.

This work is done with lightning speed and precision hour after hour. As the grueling work goes on, the men joke and banter to keep their spirits up. This work is so hard that usually only young men can do it, and only for about ten years. When an older man is unable to keep up, the others send him away because he slows them down.

After the first five hours the crew takes a half-hour lunch break. Like athletes, the men can't cool off because their muscles will tighten up. When they finish eating, it's back to work.

Señor Jesus Suarez is called *Don Chuito* by his friends. He has spent his entire life in the fields. He is now retired and he and his wife look after their grandsons while his children work.

During World War II, when the U.S. needed laborers to harvest their crops, we were hired in Mexico to come here to work as braceros. I was twenty-three years old. We were packed into freight trains and taken to Arizona to pick melons. Then we went to California to pick oranges. I liked that because I would eat lots of them. But when I got my first check, it was for only ninety cents.

The next day some of the men called out to me, "Hey big one, want to be a cargador?" Well, I wasn't doing very well as a picker so I thought I would try my luck loading trucks. My job was to throw fifty-pound boxes of lettuce up to another man who would catch them and stack them on the truck. That week my check was for thirty dollars. Now I was on my way up.

The campesinos *that come from Mexico usually come in groups. Those from Michoacan usually work the celery or lettuce. The people that come from Oaxaca work the strawberries. Those from Jalisco work on irrigation. Sometimes they try to switch to other work but they can't earn enough money for their* frijoles, *their beans.*

Then I came here to Salinas to do field work and I was happy. I sent for my wife and two daughters. Those two daughters have given me ten grandchildren. And those grandchildren have given me five great-grandchildren.

I stopped working three years ago when I was unable to keep up with the youngsters. I worked for 47 years and I retired when I was 70 years old. I ate well, slept well, con gusto. *I've picked lettuce, cauliflower, celery, carrot, melons, and oranges. The life of a bracero was good for some and sad for others. For me—why complain? People treated me well. You know that the way you treat people is the way you will be treated.*

Artichokes grow tall. To harvest artichokes a campesino carries a large bag on his back. The men work in clusters chatting as they walk up and down the rows of plants. With one hand that holds a short knife a picker reaches for an artichoke, slices it off the plant and tosses it over his shoulder into the bag. The men wear thick work gloves to protect their hands from the spiny leaves of the artichoke. When a picker's bag is full he takes it to the waiting truck, where a man lifts the bag off his shoulders and dumps the artichokes.

The foreman of this crew of Mexicans is Filipino-American, a decendant of the Asian laborers who came to this country during the late nineteenth and early twentieth centuries. Many came from China, Japan, and the Philippines to work on farms, build roads and railroads, and work the mines. They worked long and hard, saved the little they could and started businesses. When the immigration laws changed, they were allowed to bring their families here. Today this country is richer for the multicultural society that we've become.

25

Isabel Sorio is a substitute teacher.

I came from a small town with a river and all my family and friends. My father went north first and got papers for the rest of the family. I was sixteen and homesick. The language was difficult and I didn't like the school. So I returned.

The man I married took me to live on a small ranch. We didn't have money to buy food, clothes, or go to the doctor. I was pregnant and we didn't have money for the hospital. So my husband left to go north to find work. He didn't want me to go with him but I came later with the baby.

I was young and inexperienced when I started to work in the fields. I got on a crew by telling the mayordomo that I knew how to work. I was trembling all the way to the field. A young man showed me how to cut celery but the mayordomo saw me falling behind and he put me to packing. But another woman gave me a hard time so

I asked him to put me back to cutting. Then I was happy because I was able to keep up with the crew.

Eventually I went to night school. Today I work to send my son to college. I bought my house which I am paying off by sharing it with many people. I still take classes, cook, and take care of my children. Sometimes I wash clothes at midnight but I don't care. As long as I can work I'm happy. I don't want any sympathy. I have the weekends to rest, to clean the house and take the kids to the beach.

I like very much being a Mexican. I want my son to be educated and to be aware that they are Mexicans too. Because Mexicans suffer here. As far as I'm concerned slavery still exists in the United States. But nobody knows of this since nobody cuts cauliflower or celery except campesinos. Life is hard for the campesino.

Raspberries are not as hard to pick because the plants grow to the height of a person. But you still have to be careful because the canes have tiny sharp thorns. Most pickers wear gloves with cut-off fingers. A picker must be able to judge the ripeness of the fruit and pick only the ripe ones, leaving the others to ripen. A field can be harvested two or three times to get all the fruit. Around their waist pickers wear a belt that holds two buckets. When the buckets are full the picker takes them to a small shed in the middle of the field. There the berries are packed into the plastic containers that are sold in the stores.

At the end of the summer the migrant center has a *fiesta*. Martín Rodriguez, one of the parents, speaks in Spanish to the families who have come to party. "I too am a father who just came to this country. I want to urge you to take part in your children's education. Don't be afraid because we don't speak English or we work in the fields. We can adapt. We are our children's role models. There is much to take advantage of in this country. I look forward to my children succeeding," he tells the audience. "*Sí, compañeros*, we can do it."

A choral group of parents and children sings for the audience as dinner is served. It's a traditional Mexican meal of *pozole*, a stew of meat, corn, and chili. Then comes chicken with rice, beans, and tortillas.

After the meal Martín and his friend play and sing songs from the old country. They are quickly surrounded by families singing the familiar songs. There are many kisses and *abrazos* as the parents carry the sleepy children home.

In northern California, vineyards drape the rolling hills. Table grapes must be harvested with great care because they are very delicate. The *campesinos* move up and down the rows with a long wheelbarrow that holds three Styrofoam boxes. Since the grapes ripen at different times, the pickers must search among the leaves to find the ripest grapes. They snip them off with small scissors and carefully place them into boxes. Once the boxes are filled they take them to a packing shed where another worker cuts off any spoiled or imperfect grapes. The grapes are then packed into cartons that are stacked onto a pallet. A forklift will lift the pallet onto a truck to take them to market.

Farther north in Oregon the Hood River winds its way through acres and acres of apple, pear, peach, and cherry orchards. The trees in the orchards look like an orderly parade of soldiers marching across the landscape. Mount Hood towers over the fertile valley. By the end of September the peaches and cherries have been picked and it is time for the pear harvest.

The growers need migrant workers to harvest their crops. There aren't enough local workers to do the tough job, and they would charge much more than the migrants do. In order to attract experienced workers some growers offer them free housing. This keeps the same workers returning year after year.

The pickers are often an extended family or a group that comes from the same town or area of Mexico. Over the years the growers get to know their workers personally, and sometimes a grower will take his family to visit a worker's family in Mexico.

Bright green D'Anjou and other varieties of pears hang from the trees in the valley. The pickers move tall three-legged ladders from tree to tree. They climb to the top, and work their way down. Their eyes dart among the leaves, searching out the best fruit while their fingers swiftly and gently pluck the pears. Each picker carries a canvas bag into which he drops the pears. As the bag fills the picker loosens a knotted rope to deepen the bag, doubling its capacity. The bag is kept shallow at first to keep a pear from dropping too hard to the bottom and bruising. A pear that is punctured, bruised, or missing a stem will begin to rot, and the rot will spread to the other pears.

When the bag is filled the *campesino* gently spills the fruit into it a large bin. Each worker is paid by the number of bins he or she fills. A skilled picker can fill eight or nine bins a day.

A checker makes a note of which picker filled each bin. Then a tractor lifts the bin and takes it to a truck that will deliver the fruit to a packing plant.

Some field workers prefer to stay in one town rather than move on at the end of the harvest. A grower can offer additional work planting, hoeing, or pruning trees. But getting a job in a processing plant is considered by some workers a step up from working in the field. The pay is better, you don't have to stoop or climb, and you can get benefits.

At a packing plant the full bins of pears are lowered into water. The water washes and floats the fruit onto a conveyor belt, a very gentle way of moving them. The pears move between two rows of women who separate the small, off-color, or uneven pears from the best-looking ones. The rejects will be squeezed into juice.

The best pears continue on an electric conveyor that labels, weighs, and separates them into bins by size. At each bin a worker swiftly wraps each pear in tissue paper and stacks them into a box. Depending on the

size, it takes about one minute for a packer to fill a box with from eighty to one hundred pears. Since the worker is paid by the box, he or she works fast to make more money. Some pears are shipped out right away but most are stored in huge cold rooms to keep the fruit from spoiling.

Over the next six months the grower will ship the pears as the market needs them. Too much fruit in the market at the same time will lower the price. A grower works all year to raise the fruit. He is at the mercy of nature—winds, rain, drought— and the cost of machinery, chemicals, and labor. If at the end of the harvest the price of the fruit drops, he will not be able to cover his expenses or make a profit.

After the pear harvest is finished the apple harvest begins. The *mayordomo* of this orchard shows the pickers which apples to pick. Some apples will not be ripe enough, so they will be left on the tree to ripen some more. When a new person applies for work a grower will watch how he puts on his bag. The grower can tell how experienced the worker is by how well he puts the bag on.

More and more people are turning to eating produce from organic farms. Organic farmers do not use toxic pesticides. They rotate crops instead of using chemical fertilizers to keep the earth supplied with nutrients. Organic farmers raise a large variety of fruits, vegetables, and flowers. To harvest a field of turnips, *campesinos* remove the sheets of cloth that let in the rain but not the insects. Because of the variety of crops the farm grows, it can keep a crew busy almost all year.

Some small farms raise corn to sell to local markets and for their own roadside stands. This corn is picked by hand, so the picker can inspect each ear. The best ears go on the roadside vegetable stand alongside the other produce from the farm.

Señora Guadalupe Meza has worked for the same farmer for many years. She and two friends do various jobs. They pick corn and other produce by hand. Her husband, Francisco, drives a tractor for another farmer. Tonight he will work through the night harvesting corn by machine.

The Meza family has been here for many years. They own their own home, and the five children are doing well in school. The family maintains their Mexican traditions. Their son, Nicholas, and Nicholasa, one of their four daughters, dance with a Mexican folk dance group.

Some migrant families prefer to return to Mexico. Raising children without an extended family and community is difficult. Often because the parents work so much, the children are left alone. Without an extended family to look after the children, parents can lose them to gangs in the streets.

Those who stay learn English and become citizens. They try to settle in one place so they can send their children to school for the full year. Children of migrant workers often have a hard time going from one school to another. The experience can be so discouraging, many children drop out of school and go to work in the fields.

The families who stay in this country do so because they want their kids to have a good education. Then they won't have to work in the fields as their parents do. Those efforts are bearing fruit today as more children of *campesinos* become highly-educated professionals.

CESAR CHAVEZ

The better working conditions that farm workers enjoy today came mostly as a result of the work and sacrifices of César Chávez, Dolores Huerta, and the other founders of the United Farm Workers union.

César Chávez was ten years old when his father lost his small farm in Arizona. The family became migrant workers and moved to California. When he was seventeen he joined the navy and fought in World War II.

After the war César Chávez returned to dedicate his life to improving the working conditions of migrant workers.

After years of organizing farm workers the United Farm Workers Association was formed in 1962. César Chávez led the farm workers to unite and strike against the injustices they suffered. He organized nonviolent strikes. He led thousands of farm workers on marches through California to make the public aware of their plight. His followers asked the public not to buy fruits and vegetables from the growers who were the worst abusers of farm workers. When he was jailed for not calling off a *boycott* he fasted, gaining the attention of the public and the support of many of the country's leaders. The union was renamed in 1973 as the United Farm Workers of America.

The first collective bargaining agreement between farm workers and growers was signed in 1966. Union contracts required growers to provide rest periods, clean drinking water, portable toilets, hand washing facilities, and protective clothing against pesticides. They also called for an end to pesticide spraying while workers were on the fields and a ban on DDT.

The last time César Chávez fasted was in 1988. He went without eating for 36 days. He was sixty-one years old and was fasting to get the grape growers to stop spraying pesticides and to sign contracts with the union. This fast caused permanent damage to his health.

Today the union provides farm workers with health benefits, a pension plan, a hiring hall that gives seniority to workers, and low-cost housing.

César Chávez died peacefully on April 23, 1993. He was carried to the cemetery on the shoulders of his *compañeros* in a simple wooden coffin that his brother made. Fifty thousand mourners came to his funeral. On April 24, 1994, President Bill Clinton posthumously awarded him the United States Medal of Freedom. His widow, Helen, received the medal in the White House. In California, the holiday to celebrate the life of César Chávez is on March 31.

What César Chávez asked for and what the union continues to strive for are the rights and protections that are offered to other skilled industrial workers; to be treated with respect for their contributions to society; the dignity and the right to negotiate for their interests, such as a fair wage, an eight-hour day, medical and dental benefits, and protection from toxic pesticides. The union represents only a small part of the thousands of farm workers throughout the United States, and there are still abuses to be ended. *La lucha sigue!* The struggle goes on.

GLOSSARY

abrazo – an embrace, a hug

bandanna – a large multi-colored handker-chief

boycott – to not buy or deal with

bracero – day laborer

burrito – a stuffed tortilla

campesino – a farm worker

cargador – a loader, porter, stevadore

checker – a person who checks or keeps score

comal – a flat pan to cook tortillas

compañero – a companion, workmate

con gusto – with relish

coyote – a person who guides illegal aliens

don – title of respect used before first name

fiesta – festival

frijoles – beans

gracias – thank you

harvest – gathering of crops

mayordomo – foreman

migrant – a person who moves from place to place

pesticide – a chemical used to kill pests

piñata – a hanging pot filled with candies

pozole – a stew of corn, meat, and chili

señor – mister, sir

señora – lady, madam, Mrs.

tortilla – thin, cornmeal pancake

Gracias, *thanks, to all the wonderful people who helped me in my search for a story to tell: Nancy Albritton, Raul & Teresa Ayala, William Alexander, Stan & Leslie Barth, Steve Bickford, Lori De Leon, Fred Duckwall, Jose Luis Fernandez, Gathering Together Farm, Patrick Farrell, Bernice Gomez, Elia Gonzalez-Castro, Dick Keis, Oscar Marquez, Francisco & Guadalupe Meza, Alicia Fernandez Mot, Tom Nelson, Gretchen & Phil Olson, Martin Rodriquez, Dr. Jerrilyn Smith, James Sims, Isabel Soria, Jesus (Don Chuito) Suarez, Juanita Valdez-Cox, Charlotte & Yost Van Der Haven, James & Susie Wells.*

DATE